AMERICA

IN
PORTRAIT

AMERICA IN PORTRAIT

Paperback ISBN: 978-1-915223-40-1

Published by

Maurice Wylie Media
Your Inspirational & Christian Book Publisher

For more information visit
www.MauriceWylieMedia.com

Dedication

For my Grandfathers Patrick and John.

THE PATRIARCHS

For my loving Dad, Patrick.
For Uncle Peter who showed me his country.

Contents

Introduction

In my fifty or so years, it has been my privilege to journey across the four corners of the United States. Growing up as part of the third generation in Ireland's hard-won Republic, America seemed as alien to me as the moon. We caught glimpses of its skyscrapers through TV series and news broadcasts, while old black-and-white classics introduced a generation to the Wild West and its myriad intriguing characters—some wise, others burdened by misfortune. Through the screen and the exploits of literary heroes, I suppose I fell in love with America before ever setting foot there. Unlike many of our ancestral European kin, my generation has enjoyed the freedom to travel, albeit within the bounds of financial constraints.

In his seminal essay The Fate of Empires, author John Glubb outlines the foundational traits and cyclical progression of historical empires. His thesis argues that each empire begins with a period of venturesome fortitude and pioneering spirit. Glubb demonstrates how this initial fervour wanes over time as comfort and entitlement take root, inevitably leading to decline. The average lifespan of an empire, he asserts, is approximately 250 years, with its downfall often heralded by the rise of a competitor. This pattern is as old as history itself. A study of Biblical accounts reveals the rise and fall of numerous civilizations—blessings for obedience and curses for dishonour—as early societies flourished and then wept for nourishment amid their decline.

The parallels between Ireland's new Republic and America's history are not distant; they are deeply intertwined. Escaping the past requires vision, fortitude, courage, resilience, hard work, and determination. Blood and sacrifice are often necessary as new lands and opportunities are developed, eventually giving rise to distinct cultures and traditions. These short stories, songs, and poems offer insight into the complexity of human relationships: the striving for security, the pursuit of opportunity, the hunger, passion, and avarice for success, the bonds of family, the voice of love, and the resonant growl of thunder. Beneath the surface, under the veneer of cultural differences, lies a universal truth—we are all the same, shaped by the foundation of time itself.

This is the story of every nation, as we live in what are indeed interesting times.

Part 1

1600 - 1799

Fortitude

SOUTH CAROLINA SHORE – MARCH 1607

What if the three ships were joined by a fourth?

It was December 1606 and I, just sixteen, set upon a new commission.
Leaving kin, friend and foe for adventure,
we sailed, a convoy of Mayflower four:
Susan Constant, Godspeed, Discovery and Fortitude,
we despatched with hope and full measure of fear.
Till March, Year of our Lord 1607, we charted strong
I toiling in sunshine, squall hail and at times
a climate of complete abandon,
till one day pox was found on "Fortitude".
We then set adrift, rudderless and cannon-balled
all found asleep but I;
our ship and hope set aflame and downward sunk.

Midst last death breath, through frenzied urgency
I launched forth toward a faint compass of sunlight
spotted through bleak ocean depth.
In the last seconds of sense and thought born reason
scrambling fingers secured air,
scraping a dislodged and rescuing plank.
This mighty behemoth floating by self
bobbed with restless impatience as if its
sole aspiration was my company.
I clambered heavily upon this Jonah's salvation
with misery tear and forced gulped breath.
Death point passed but not yet extinguished
for sanctuary was still unseen across
tumult's wild white-topped horizon.

Three days hence, adrift and holding fast
tired and hungry, westward I spied
fair shoreline of South Caroline.
I endeavoured the last fathom stretch
with punishing wretchedness,
a solitary hand clasping beach line sand.
I hauled myself to tree cluster whereby I fought for return of strength
gorging nature's reserve: fruit, leaf and hard soil crop.

Starburst ablaze became my guiding night sky.
I northward on foot set pace
toward the Mayflower settlement,
my mind confirming that the same
fortitude and courage would be required
to prosper and advance in this new land.

All but One Day

OREGON SHORELINE – SOMETIME AROUND 1652

It always rains in Oregon.

Twelve colored stones
dressed like a pillar,
touching; one against the other,
ocean cascade.
Sea current pulling under,
rumble of thunder,
shore grass all a flutter,
wind brushed, mist and haze.
Dark sky, no horizon,
cloud travelling;
deep blues, blacks and grey.

Land distant looks foreboding,
redwood shelter,
salt smell linger,
shore swept shells.
Bounding waves,
iridescent tops
falling slowly
added to by rain and hail.

No time, no day
no month, no date.
Wet rain falling
always the same.
Oregon shoreline
rugged, beautiful,
sublime.

One day though
the sun broke through.
Not good; made it all look the same.
Don't worry,
won't last long,
tomorrow's promise
will bring back rain.

Against the Grain

NEW ORLEANS, LOUISIANA - 1767

Prosper together or die in vain.

Each man made a conscious decision to let the other live. Instead of murder, though at a time of uprising it would have been judged an act of war, the men deliberately chose to find common ground. Stumbling between native tongues mixed with pigeon English alliance was forged by a shared interest in lumber.

Prior to insurrection against Spanish trading rights, Frenchman Pierre Lebois and Spaniard David Cortez eked out a living swinging ragged axe as weather-beaten lumbermen. The Louisiana and the Mississippi basin provided a humid heavy verdant green five hundred mile stretch of prize wood. With wildlife to survive upon, European blood cut, sawed and fought for rights across the vast fertile delta swathe. Mutiny, carnage and plain old murder were commonplace as tradition bound settlers sought individual and collective opportunity midst the sweat grill of bayou swamp.

Lebois and Cortez fought in one such skirmish. Savage blows were both delivered and received then lying side by side in a blood drench clasp they realised the futility of violence. Both men decided to enter an economic partnership. Virgin ground was broken in New Orleans, the men constructing a foundry and timber-mill with monies secured at a temperate rate. Over the years willow, birch, sycamore, spruce, hardwood maple, cherry and pine red oak passed through iron saw and hammer. The necessary implements of water, fire, boil and spit provided by the majestic river and hard labor harnessed the belts and grindstone that split Louisiana nature into buildable plank. The forest's leafy floor was transformed into wooden wall in town and city across the southern state.

Business flourished as New Orleans became the entry and exit point for the new nation's early industry and farming heartland export to the old world: barge and ship transferring cotton and tobacco into gold.

In the time of Spanish ascendancy Cortez chaired the company transferring responsibility to Lebois on French succession in the early 19th century. The partnership became a template for co-operation in an era of international revolution. Harmony and unity established and fashioned economically out of potential disarray and violent dysfunction.

Wandering Whisper – Totem Carver

NEVADA TERRITORY 1775

Don't let detractors eradicate a rich heritage.

What I hear is the tale I tell,
carved in wood; painted then.
Shadowed eyes, my sight long dark,
my ears hear the stories I sculpt in bark.

Rhythm by rhythm, listen; nature's sound,
bird song echo, wild beast growl.
Rugged hilltop, lone stand tree,
melting river, rock blast scree,
ice pack scavenge, forest line run,
rain drop puddle, mountain path sun.
Hail shower pelt, windswept chant,
thunder shout clap, seasons advance.......

Village by village, tent by tent,
from breathing landscape to tribe blood dance.
Apache, Navajo, Cheyenne, Sioux;
Pawnee, Cherokee, Shawnee, Crow.
Prairie plain to desert scorch trail,
hammer, chisel, measure piece and nail.
Discovering history I leave with my mark,
listening to understand, carved slowly in bark.

Hear what is hidden, hear what is said,
hearing laughter in life, hearing sorrow in death.
Subtle nuances captured in kinship pole,
conversations by fireside warmed by night coal.

War time heroes of victories ago,
embellished adventures and a future in flow,
learning to hunt and learning to throw,
Elders teaching....... patient.......slow.

Nation by kingdom, I came and I left,
rich ancestry, the proud and the spent.
Listening to work, while there they would care,
helping me move to here then to there.
Wandering Whisper they called me by name,
my people, my culture but never the same.

A wood carved tale over time will erode,
it's the story it leaves that gets ingrained in the soul.

Part 2

1800 - 1899

The Testing of Abraham Slew

MARSH LAKE, MINNESOTA - 1841

Miracles occur when the anointed listen and obey.

The teams of wood and iron axled creaking wheels worked their
physic propelling the canvass-topped wagons westward. The caravan of
Scandinavian stock, compassed toward the mid-west, first forged river
and springtime mountain pass; each wheel turns leaving a hungry past
directed them toward a promised tomorrow.

Dirty and oblivious laughing children ran happily aside.
Rusted tin and utensil clanked, dogs skulked and foraged,
while grown kin bravely pondered; concern etched upon granite faces.
Water a plenty but food was dangerously short.
Preacher Abraham Slew, though confidence waning,
feigned a mantle of warm security exhorting that
The Lord Himself would provide a coveted ram for His people.

Earlier that season over one thousand miles away in the north-western
Rocky Mountains the suspended ice waterfalls had thawed.
Broken ice and snow melt had begun to empty into the enterprise
of the Mississippi tributaries. Flowing momentum brought vast quantities
of fresh water and life into Marsh Lake.

It was there that Abraham Slew spotted the annual migrating dance and
orchestrations of white feathered, yellow beaked Pelican. Thousands of
white heads dipped to gorge upon mighty carp, trout and salmon.
Abraham pointed to the free gift: a veritable underwater treasure trove.
Tensions eased immediately. The adults laughed too like carefree children.
Abraham Slew bowed in prayerful contemplation and thanksgiving.
The journey could for a time, rest.

Faith and coincidence are poor neighbours. Their respective pulls and emotions are at constant enmity with each other.
Faith tested and proved, Abraham Slew sought further instruction.

In the century up to 1925, one-third of Norway's population emigrated westward to new opportunity.

Old Story in a New Land

SOUTHWEST NEBRASKA – 1855

It is difficult to forget the past.

The long journey around the mountain would take serious navigation and time so the "SAVE TOO WEKS – TOLLL ONLY $5" sign secured Londoner John Ramsey Etheridge's attention as he steered his wagon westward. His older brother had written to inform him of the shortcut and Etheridge halted his wagon, smiling in anticipation of the encounter. Scotsman R. McIntosh emerged from his rough and tumble well well-worn wooden toll booth.

"Are you the four-toothed, yellow-bellied R. McIntosh who has the three brothers further up your private trail?" quizzed Etheridge. A slight nod of the head confirmed the questioner's suspicions.

"Is your older brother the R. McIntosh who charges unsuspecting fools $5 each for a ferry ride across the North Platte a day's wheel up your land?" the refined voice queried. McIntosh stood silent as Etheridge continued. "And is he your brother the R. McIntosh who charges again for the campsite two days from here?"

McIntosh was seething, perspiration flowed down his petulant face but knowing that his brothers hated Englishmen as much as he a thin smile unveiled. This guy would soon be stopped by a bullet! But first he'd extract his $5 and one of his brothers would finish the job. Better to hide the evidence in the wilderness.

"Is your last brother the younger R. McIntosh who owns the provision store that extorts further unsuspecting idiots?" Etheridge confidently resumed still awaiting a verbal response to his first query. "It would surprise most that your shortcut costs over $50 and saves people only 4 days." Etheridge's final flourish was designed to provoke an attack.

McIntosh smiled revealing three dirty yellow hunks of enamel. "Oh! I thought you had four teeth you miserable Scottish vagabond?" exclaimed the Londoner.

"Had till last week you pompous Sassenach. Lost one of them while I was chewing a bullet," the rugged Glaswegian snarled. "Who informed you anyways?" demanded McIntosh. "My brother wrote," came the curt reply.

"Tell you what you dozy Limey. You keep quiet about our enterprise and I'll just take $5 en I'll give you a token which will afford you free passage with my kin," the canny Scot appealed while simultaneously doffing his hat.

Etheridge agreed, paid his toll and accepted the token. Further verbal assaults were exchanged as the old country neighbours parted company. Both men laughed each claiming victory as the wagon disappeared out of sight.

Etheridge called to his hiding companion: his own younger brother. "J.R one of these McIntosh's will want to avenge history for his countrymen and unless we shoot first we'll end up dead. We'll have to shoot all three brothers and hope it takes time for that first guy to find out. If we do this properly we'll cut the ferry ropes and he'll have no way to cross the river. At that stage, we'll be long gone."

J.R looked fondly at his older brother. "Father was correct when he warned us. Never trust a Scotsman when you're awake and be doubly awake when you're asleep."

The wagon rolled on toward the next encounter.

The Agitators

DUBUQUE, IOWA – 1858

Where you find man, plotting and division are always close by!

Investor Clayton Burrows' patience had run thin as he glared at his two business partners. His finances had been drained, he having lost hundreds of thousands of dollars in the previous year's economic downturn. The current argument centred upon Iowa's Shot Tower; an intriguing building that facilitated the manufacture of lead bullets. Lead was dropped from a height through a grating system. On descent the lead would form spheres; they in turn would cool in cold water at the tower's base. Each cooled unit formed a perfect bullet.

"I thought your lead bullet manufacturing idea to be one of my more exciting and potentially profitable investments. I was happy to commence building your Shot Tower but like all projects you two are involved in the costs escalated. Initially you asked me to fund a 50-foot tower, but that didn't form the spheres, then you tried 70 feet, then 100 feet. We completed the tower topping out at 120 feet; four times the allocated budget. But the biggest problem we have is that after manufacturing over one million bullets," his voice rising practically beyond comprehension, "WE HAVE NO WAR AND I WANT MY MONEY!"

Scandinavian Erikson was more practised at hiding his anger. He let his companion rant while he formulated a reasonable response and at an appropriate time he interjected. "Well Clayton, like back home in Europe we'll just have to manufacture a conflagration of epic proportion. It will be easier here as a division already exists with the Mason-Dixon line." The added dimension silenced Burrows and the third partner.

"You're right Clayton, the world seems pretty quiet at the moment but history demonstrates that war is always on the horizon. Reckon we'll have to create division and we can commence by agitating the southerner. Agitate them and agitate them some more; there is nothing as angsty as an agitated southerner. They're like unwieldy red-headed foals jumping to scratch someone else's itch. We'll just agitate that itch until it's raw and believe me they'll scratch."

Like a descending piece of lead Clayton Burrows cooled and intensified his concentration. He beckoned Erikson to continue. "As for the northerners, well they think they're refined and cultured. Already half of them think they're Frenchmen! In truth they're hotheads; mostly Irish and Scots and a heady mix of both. Worse than any Italian; the smell of a fight is good enough."

Clayton and Marsden smiled and Erikson knew his reasoning and quest would prevail. "Those northerners," he continued "hit before they think and if we can find an Englishman in the midst the whole tower will collapse, no pun intended!! If we can agitate all that, well.....we'll have momentum and fusion. I'll tell you one thing Clayton; your million bullets will not be enough. So Marsden can you ramp up production, Burrows you do the selling and boys I'll do the agitating. We'll create such an itch that when both sides decide to scratch we'll be there to provide the ointment."

"What if they come to destroy our new tower?" voiced concerned Burrows.

"We're just far enough away to survive," remarked a casual Erikson. "They'll enjoy the fighting too much to be concerned with us. We'll only be in trouble if Marsden can't supply enough ongoing fuel. Whatever's left at the end of the war we'll just sell to whoever wants to fight elsewhere."

Marsden walked slowly to the cabinet. He poured three measures of brandy and raised a toast to war.

Stars, Stripes and Blood.

MONTGOMERY, ALABAMA 1863

Each and all carry a dignity.

300 miles from cotton, 300 miles to his dream,
300 miles by moonlight running through valley and stream.
300 miles to the battle outmanoeuvring owners behind,
300 miles from family, with each step a memory died.

Tom Slave No Second Name left Alabama wondering if he would ever return.
Believing in a greater destiny,
he could not accept emancipation unless he too played his part.
Freedom won by others would be a gift; won by himself his responsibility.
Owned by plantation but free inside, the battle that commenced in his mind
took shape upon Tom Slave No Second Name's first step escape toward liberty.

300 miles from cotton, 300 miles to his dream.

Alabama flowed though Tom's veins though he donned Union blue.
He fought for freedom and sometimes vengeance.
He fought for his God, thinking that some are created in His image.
Milliken's Bend, Port Hudson, Petersburg etched in memory
where now Tom Freeman His Own Second Name both drew and lost blood,
each step circumventing martyr's grave and numbered cross.

300 miles to battle, 300 miles from his past.

Through hell fire the cannon fodder ran and fell.
Brother with brother, maimed and dead.
Bullet by bullet, shell by shell,
no creed, no color, in this savaged hell,
striving, surviving
till at Fort Wagner Tom Freeman His Own Second Name fell.

300 miles from family till even that memory died.

At Wagner, Tom Freeman His Own Second Name had carried the flag,
thirty-five stars drenched in a nation's loss,
thirty-five stars now displaying the red of Tom Freemans's blood.

That flag was sent to his mother and years later it became her shroud.
300 miles from her lifeblood, thirty-five stars buried proud.

Hard Scrabble

BLACKFOOT, IDAHO TERRITORY - 1864

My Aunt Noreen gave me this title; she is one of the bravest people I know.

The Ireland of 1848 served two foreign masters; the empirical British crown and the black-clad corridors of Rome which demanded allegiance over Monarch. Subservient to both, yet loyal to neither Ireland's fierce countenance compassed the nation toward a future independence. Circumstances contrived and famine ravaged the Isle of rugged windswept beauty. The full extent of potato blight and the wilful neglect of both sovereigns led to the unchartered massacre of over one million souls with forced emigration expelling an equal number.

Hard pressed and malnourished, potato farmer Myles McCarthy and his wife left Clonakilty in County Cork and walked the near fifty miles to Cove Harbour for passage to America on one of the hundreds of coffin ships that transported a million to the land of new opportunity. Dreadful unsanitary conditions compressed the weary and beaten together while stench, brutality and disease claimed the weak. Myles' wife passed too, her remains given reverently by him to the roiling ocean which heaved in a tempest of perpetual greyness.

New York did not provide Myles' hoped for salvation. He was deposited within the disembarked hoards and then housed in a ram-shackled tenement that made uneasy neighbour with hate, suspicion and fear. Advantage was easily taken and his meagre dollars were dwindled by the cunning deceit of earlier settlers. Myles, a country lad at heart, took flight of brick and headed west; his quest, a small farm and maybe new wife. He trekked for 18 months, working to feed and travel. Clonakilty's much loved son was seeking the perfect soil; ground that he hoped would never again disappoint and devastate.

Idaho provided that haven. The Idaho Territory combined the perfect altitude mix of sunshine, mineral enhanced dark rich soil with suitable irrigation provided from the spring snowmelts of north western mountain ranges. A new homestead was constructed and Myles specialist knowledge on potato cultivation was invested. Myles married a local Blackfoot daughter and a son was born the following year. Myles once again belonged and he became a popular member of the interdependent community. Memories of Ireland and earlier cruel days grew fainter with every passing year. Idaho became home.

The harvest of 1862 failed and blight hit in 1863. Myles, like his first wife, passed into oblivion, the same rich Idaho soil becoming his resting place.

The Noble Advancement of Good

SPRINGFIELD – ILLINOIS 1865

Come the hour, riseth the leader

The water worked through the hardest of times
flatboat barge navigating the Springfield spine,
young man travelling, steer pole in hand
watching the trading; one selling, one buying.
Attentive ears picking up quayside noise
the barter, the chatter, the truth and lies;
discerning spirits, the mean and the good
adding to knowledge he gleaned from his books.

Language skills grew, soon came to the fore
stood in the breach for the rich and the poor.
Reputation gathered merit and pace,
Lawyering and politic both found their place.
Through personal tragedy came noble call,
life in service for others, soon City Hall.

There comes an hour, there comes a time
brave men must stand, eyes open wide.
A vision for nation, shaped by eras lost days,
understanding his people from living their ways,
foundation forged; character not led by hearsay.

Bitter struggle cauldron in this century land
brothers often fighting, killing hand to hand.
Solomon's wisdom delivering hard choice,
decisions tough requiring clear voice.
Lifeblood of future, hope kept to the fore
freedom for every man in union against foe.

Fragile this Eden, first fruit to abound,
though Abel's blood once again poured to the ground.
One hundred years hence MLK due same fate,
no exodus, just sleep till trumpet from heaven's own gate.
In a struggle toward destiny, courage and valour stand forth,
they shine through a beacon; safe harbour of hope.

Trojan Bear

ALASKA – 1866

Rather than look in the mirror it is often easier to blame outside influence.

Known for his probing intelligence and strategic vision Tsar Alexander's rich and authoritative voice held a steady determined pace as he announced what he personally believed would be a crowning achievement and defining legacy. The audience, gathered in Alexander's Moscow Palace, sat in silence, some out of reverence, some fearful, while ambitious others nodded obsequious approval.

"In the not-too-distant future," he continued, "I fear our beloved glorious imperial monarchy and kingdom will, in the name of freedom be replaced by a decaying philosophical entropy. As I speak I observe the Judas cauldron that dare to plot even in our midst. I would remind them that civilised leaders do not execute dissenting thinkers. I am content enough that if they examine their preached doctrine they will soon surmise its folly and end.

America though will emerge as the next pre-eminent world power. Their defining civil war will bolster federal union and they have now what every aspiring nation requires: a martyred leader, a hero to rally their phoenix. United, they will rise to build unprecedented industry, wealth and military prowess: national strengths which we need to shape into our image. It is my fervent desire to sell them Alaska at a price they cannot ignore. The money is immaterial as we will reap reward into the coming decades and centuries. In Russia, as my few American friends say, we play the long game: we sitting here today will not gain the advantage of future generations. We will settle a remnant in Alaska who will be educated to our strategic aim and they, with full citizenship rights, will be directed into the diplomatic, political and intelligence services. We will leave the day-to-day functioning of America to nations of no ambition and strategic importance. The ordinary will always exist; the extraordinary will emerge over time." Tsar Alexander II left the stage to tremendous applause.

In October 1867, just one year later, Alaska was sold to the American Government for $7.2 million: just 2 cent an acre.

Safely secured behind private doors Alexander directed his chosen few confidants to identify opportunity and prepare similar plans for South America, the Caribbean and the Pacific islands. The learning from the Alaskan enterprise would be applied with rigorous and far reaching intent.

The Rich Man and Lazarus

PROMONTORY SUMMIT – UTAH, MAY 1869

East and West collided on a railway track.

The Railway Director removed the golden spike from the safe
and made his way toward his Chairman at the VIP platform.
En route he passed two men carrying a shroud-covered stretcher.
"What will we do with him; he's dead?" they queried.
"Throw it in the ditch with the offal," came the curt, snarled response.
"At least get the Preacher!" the braver railroad navvy beseeched.
"No, it was heathen. Anyways the Preacher is officiating later," the
Director roared as he stumbled hurriedly toward the opening of the
transcontinental line.

At 12:47pm on a crisp May afternoon the spike was ceremoniously
hammered; the occasion immortalised in Andrew J. Russell's photograph.
Captured within was the Director's smiling face, he flush with the
anticipation of future wealth.

Rather than fight in the Nian Rebellion of the 1860's, the newly
qualified doctor, Ching Tsien, escaped China making a difficult path to
the port of Hong Kong. He foraged for meagre rations, sleeping when
possible in wooden sheds and foliage covered ditches. He worked for
food and board on a returning Pacific Mail Steamship, arriving in San
Francisco in the Fall of 1867.

The Promised Land held nothing but hate and contempt for the
millions of immigrants who landed in various ports. The stress of the
previous twelve months took a heavy toll on Ching's fragile mental
and physical strength but he secured a wage labouring for the Central
Pacific Railroad Company. Mile after mile Ching toiled, lifting steel

and lumber; he sometimes shovelling 20 pounds of rock over 400 times a day. Paid less than the white workers, Ching lived with his fellow Chinese in tents enduring horrendous conditions in every element.

It all ended upon that last day. Expectant of celebration Ching was instead hit by a runaway rail cart. His death crept upon him slowly, he dying from a crushed spine and skull; his doctor's brain smashed beyond repair. For his grave they cast him aside without ceremony and without a marker. Ching lies there alone to this day.

Upwards of 15,000 Chinese workers helped build the transcontinental railroad. The majority never saw their homeland again. Their parents held cherished memories, most not even having a photograph of their much-beloved children.

Not All as it Seems

PHOENIX, ARIZONA – 1869

For my son Luke, a modern-day adventurer

Renowned photographer John Karl Hillers entered the studio in the newly settled sweltering Phoenix. The tinkling bell announced his arrival to proprietor Shaw Hardcoop who left the back room to engage a potential customer. Hillers was staggered at Hardcoop's near seven foot tough looking rugged frame, inwardly believing that he had found his man; a strong looking man at that.

"Mr. Hardcoop?" he inquired offering his hand. "I'm J.K Hillers, JK to my friends and I'd like to make you a once in a lifetime proposal." Hardcoop stood motionless and beckoned the stranger to continue.

"Well Mr. Hardcoop, or can I call you Shaw?" to which he didn't receive a reply. " Well......Mr. Hardcoop, I am part of the Powell Geographic Expedition team that will later this year chart the entire Grand Canyon and we are looking for a ....em, a strong, determined photographer to join the team. We were informed that you Shaw....sorry, Mr. Hardcoop are indeed the best photographer in Phoenix ..are you Mr. Hardcoop ....the best in Phoenix?"

"Oh! I don't know about that," replied Hardcoop.

"Actually not only Phoenix, we believe you to be the best photographer in all Arizona!" Hillers stated excitedly to who he believed was the finest physical specimen of a man he had ever seen. The tough extremity of the expedition would be chicken feed to this remarkable giant.

"Oh! I don't know about that," responded the towering behemoth. "Will it be cold and will I have to get wet?"

Hillers looked staggered and couldn't believe his ears. "Well Mr. Hardcoop ....em...a journey like this has never been done before. I do believe we will get wet crossing the Colorado River. Does the prospect excite you?"

"Oh! I don't know about that," Hardcoop replied. "Will I have to sleep outside under the open sky? I don't like sleeping outside, only did it the once."

"But look at the size of you Mr. Hardcoop and how intimidating you are," an exasperated Hillers responded doing his best to contain his emotion.

"Oh! I don't know about that," Hardcoop said shifting his bulk against the studio counter.

"Ah Mr. Hardcoop," roared Hillers. "Are you not excited about potentially photographing the Canyon for the very first time? Can you not imagine the adventure, the fun with the team, the tough work, the........Mr. Hardcoop, are you a man or a ...."

"A mouse," interjected Hardcoop. "I've said it Hillers to save you face. I'm a mouse Mr. Hillers. Sorry to say it: a mouse. Reckon you'll have to look elsewhere but as you know Arizona only has a few of us photographers."

"Have you anything...I mean anything to say, Mr. Hardcoop?" an increasingly angry Hillers demanded.

"Oh! I don't know about that. Yes in fact I do J.K. Both our second names begin with H!" Hardcoop smiled like he had made a scientific discovery.

J.K. Hillers left dejected, disappointed that he had lost his temper but in many ways pleased that Hardcoop was not joining them. It would have been a chore to nurse him. Hillers put the incident out of mind and returned to the team to undertake one of the most breathtaking journeys of all time.

The giant locked the door disappointed that he had to reject what he felt was the most incredible opportunity he had ever been offered. He returned to the backroom where a meek and timid Shaw Hardcoop sat heavily bound and gagged.

"Well did you get rid of him?" Jesse James inquired. "Or did you have to shoot him?"

"He's gone," replied the disappointed henchman now yearning for pure rugged geographic adventure. "He's gone and he's not coming back."

"Great. Let's get back down to business." encouraged James.

J.K. Hillers had indeed found his man but The Outlaw had found him first.

Yellowstone Eagle

WYOMING MARCH 1872

Nothing like an eagle in timeless full wing

Streamlined trajectory
o'er vast blue sky,
waterfall canyons
white glacial lines.
Hued forest canvass,
hibernations awake,
focused fierce sharpness
through springtime snowflake.

Rocky outcrop sentinel
launching from perch-top tor,
golden feathers,
thermal soar.
Talons and tendons
nature's sword,
patrolling surroundings
harvesting food.

Tenacious majesty
regal gaze,
surveying domain
nursing fledging babes.
Nest choir flutter
feeding beak,
getting stronger
sky soon to streak.

Flight on the wings of an Eagle
floating in this mysterious place,
all is calm
in this heavenly peace.

Ten Cliff High

COLORADO 1873

Hey Blarkey! Heres to the next Flatiron adventure.

Horse clop trot through Burnt Ridge Vine,
lone rider, fixed granite stone and lime.
Sweat brow boil as sun rides high,
stooped movement, cadenced rhyme.
One intent,
one to die.

Ten Cliff High, Ten Cliff High,
one born to live, one born to die.
Maelstrom pending,
breath soon ending
who'll be last standing
at Ten Cliff High.

Town approaches,
hear the death bell toll,
no rest be taken
till my will be done.
Pace path beaten under clock tower turn,
street silent,
vengeance gripping cold steel gun.

Ten Cliff High, Ten Cliff High,
one born to live, one born to die
who'll be last standing
at Ten Cliff High.

Clock ticking down
circling dance,
shadowed observers
brave in distance.
Odds agreed,
coins soon to pass.
heart slows down
no last chance.

Ten Cliff High, Ten Cliff High.

Time stands still at Ten Cliff High
unmarked grave where one'll reside,
no room in heaven for a hell bound son,
trigger cocked, bullet ready; just need one.
Repentance can be sought another day,
redemption for one just moments away.

Ten Cliff High, Ten Cliff High,
who'll be last standing at Ten Cliff High.

Sixty seconds in this rugged plain.
Sixty seconds from dust crop grain.
Sixty seconds to extract disaster.
Sixty seconds; gut rot slaughter.

Ten Cliff High, Ten Cliff High.

Head hung low,
lone rider leaves,
mountains beckon,
rivers and trees.
It's a lifetime plan to chase a man,
sixty seconds to knock him down,
sixty seconds in Ten Cliff High
sixty seconds, blood-soaked ground.

There's no escape from hardened death,
a wanted poster
sky pointed feet.
Shadows emerge
tongues will tattle
life goes on,
this now a forgotten battle.

Today Valkyrie sojourned at Ten Cliff High,
one born to live,
one born to die.

Ruthless Men Retain Riches

OKLAHOMA – APRIL 22, 1889

Shrewd thinkers always seem to survive.

The wicked Jed Arthurs barged angrily into the room and stared down his four equally unrighteous sons.

"ListenenUp," Jed hollered. "Dis is whats we's en youse is gonna do. Wher peoples gathers thats whers de moneys gathern toos en we's got myself a plan to builds us a clan die-nasty. Listenen up ya hears! Next week theys gonna give free land yonder abroad Oklahoms ways en y'awl youse goona stake us claims.

Three y'awl brothers head out afore date and set camp by Kingfisher Creek up Lisbon ways. April twenty-too youse three claim yers 160 acres eachum. I be's in city with Hal here; we's do de rest. Circle another 80 acres both sides de creek's edge which Hal will claim later sames day.

Takems withya Winchester Repeaters to fend off any those clawbellies come up nears our land. Shoot ta kill dem ya hears me! Shoots ta kill."

The three sooners headed out to execute the plan and any "clawbellies" stupid enough to interfere. Time journeyed on too and the following week arrived.

Thirty minutes before high noon, Jed, Hal and three similarly clad farmhands stood outside the newly opened Oklahoma Sheriff's Office and had their picture stills taken for the local newspaper. Jed later paid $20 for copies of the grainy black and white slightly distorted portrait of the vaguely familiar shaped clan.

At 12 noon sharp a canon blasted and mayhem ensued. Dust, sweat and murder unleashed speedily from the blocks and headed west. Horse and wagon tore the ground asunder but at a much slower pace than the wished intent. 50,000 hopeful trailblazers staked identity poles over 2 million acres of previously owned Native American heartland.

Hal roared a four horse relay toward his brother's enclave and Jed claimed 160 just north of the Oklahoma City boundary. The three "sooner" brothers shot and killed several "clawbellies" who attempted to breach their rich soil defences. Later that day five Arthur's claims were registered. At a subsequent trial of suspected fraudsters Jed produced his black and whites: proof that all five were in Oklahoma City just before the canon blast. The case was dismissed. The Arthur's celebrated hard and heavy that night.

"I payed them suckers $100 each to stand in thatum photo still," Jed smugly chuckled to his sons. "Havin Hal standin there in the middle o thems was just jenius......pure jenius!!"

The Arthurs farmland produced and supplied fruit and crops to the burgeoning city. Their city acres formed the first industrial and warehouse site in the entire State; the fifty miles between facilitated ease of conveyance.

"Bars, dinge joints en clubs will comes en go's," recorded Jed in his die-nasty memoirs, "but folks a gathern new places always needs to everydays eats."

Leave your Mark

BLACKHILLS, SOUTH DAKOTA - 1891

History too has a past.

The only sounds were the growling stomachs as the four residents of nearby Keystone made camp for the approaching night. The weekend hunting trip had so far been successful and a hastily prepared stew was cooking over the hot fire flame. As they waited the older man regaled his companions with stories of the early century fur trapper mountainmen. He spoke of harsh beaten bearded and chiselled characters of yore and their skill with single-shot flintlock and bowie knife. The listeners were mesmerised with tales of eye trained scouts, the shared encounters with native tribes, stories of tough land foe and of course the coveted prize; the short hair insulated pelt required for rich men's fashion.

One of the younger men lit the oil lanterns and in the fading light he gasped as he looked up at the jagged stripped back rock of earth crust bone. "Look at that guys!" he exclaimed and pointed. "Is it just me or does that mountain outcrop look like a head?" The others mooched over from the warming coals.

"Ya, you could sculpt that if you were so inclined," came the reply. "All you'd need is time and a whole lot of money. Who would you prop up on that pedestal?"

"You could engineer the President's head up there," one of the four proposed.

"No way!" the older storyteller laughed. "Why he's all the way over there in Washington; may as well be in another country. We've more in common with the farming stranger in Australia," he mused.

"I know....I'd love to see Abigail Grube in all her glory up there," the youngest man offered. The others went silent as they contemplated Keystone's beauty.

"Stop now boys. We should immortalise your mother up there for all she's done for you; the trials you put her through as teenagers.....ya, your mother it is. Lets have our supper and Dan you get the cards out. Reckon we have about an hour before the dark settles in for the night. Ya they've hills within mountains here," the aged man concluded as the hunters returned to the fire. Four bowls of foraged meat and beans were split amongst the family and each man ate hungrily after the long day: their promise, a similar tomorrow.

Mouths remained silent as each man took in the purplish blue red tinged flame and noisy crackle of fresh cut wood. The unique aroma scent of century old branch added a lazy perceptible taste to the hunt meat stew. These frequent golden moments of company and story would remain locked in respective memories; a tale to be told to a future generation. Like life, the bluish grey vapour of burning wood smoke ascended to the far flung starry heavens.

Esau and Jacob Akers

PANHANDLE, TEXAS 1898

The lure of adventure and the lure of money.

"Youse can lern by reedin buks
or youse can lern by doin,"
Esau son of Amos Akers wud say.
Standing on stirrups
Esau would survey the family's 1,200 head of pure Texan Longhorn Steer.
The Panhandle ranch had all he and many future Akers would ever need.

"If'in its in ya itching ta get out
youse just got ta let it stray,"
Esau son of Amos Akers wud say.
He left early one morning and
journeyed through the spine of America.
He slept outdoors,
observing wild starlight expanse,
eating with strangers,
enjoying the friendly banter of fireside jokes.
Steely gritted determination directed toward yellow gold.

"Vanity of vanities.
Repent for the Kingdom of Heaven is at hand,"
the Preacher used to implore each Sabbath morn
but Esau always slept on the hard wooden pew.
"I reeds nature not buks,"
Esau son of Amos Akers wud say.
The cold killed Esau one night
on a lonesome Kenai mountain-top pass;
he was within grasping distance of his Yukon dream.

Many said after that it was the allure and lust
of what he already had that killed him.
Esau was 28 years old.

"He just upp'd n left likes the fool he was,"
Amos son of Seth Akers wud say.

Black gold was discovered on Akers' land a decade later.
Months later the first Model T left Detroit
and the Akers' future was set forever secure.
Amos son of Seth Akers worked and harvested oil until he too died.
Jacob, younger brother of Esau Akers, inherited.

"As he came from his mother's womb,
naked shall he return.
To go as he came;
and he shall take nothing from his labour
which he can carry away in his hand."

This also resides in The Lord's Holy Buk.

Part 3

1900 – 1999

Ill Gotten Gains

MONTANA 1902

There be a way to use a second chance and there be a way not to.

The first time Bill Riker saw Montana
occurred when he was dangling from a rope some twenty feet high
and from a neighbouring State which he had never left.
He thought Montana looked beautiful
and his last thought before entering eternity
was what life might have been like over yonder in Montana.
It was only then that Sheriff Charles Boone spoke.

Christened William J. Riker, William hated his first name
thinking it too formal: Billy too childlike.
Bill Riker was his preference and he became one of the
most furtive, secretive criminals that part of the world ever knew.
Bill Riker, who never carried a gun, amassed a fortune of millions.
Specialising in "crimes of the mind,"
he left a trail of fraud, deceit, embezzlement
and lawman bewilderment in his wake.

The Fowler's snare, as designed, will always catch.
Bored one night and in need of excitement, Bill joined a rustler's gang
and ended up alone in the hands of Sheriff Boone.
"Don't worry William," Boone sneered, rising his bait,
"We'll give you a fair trial before we hang you!"
Bill was furious; no one had called him William
since his mother and she had abandoned him.
Boone knew this and extracted his advantage.

It was there hanging twenty feet high,
outsmarted by this equally cunning foe, that Bill made his deal.
Sheriff Boone and two deputies left with Riker's fortune
while Bill was lowered and allowed walk the short five miles to Montana.
Boone was found smiling six months later shot to death in a house of ill repute.
Soon after, penniless Bill became a politician and was later appointed
Senator for his new home State: Montana.
He died ten years later, a millionaire again
having defrauded both his adoring voters and the Federal Government alike.
Ill gotten gains might entice in their pursuit
but those who get a second chance hardly ever use it for good.

No Guts, No Glory

KITTY HAWK, NORTH CAROLINA – 1903

A Kitty Hawk squall at three in the morning is invigorating.

As he later reflected it was all the fault of an annoying mosquito. Laying in bed as a young eleven-year-old the unrelenting buzz and air assault of an odious mosquito propelled Wills Lipscomb out of the house and down toward the outer banks shoreline. The family home was ideally situated within the miles of flat shoreline and home to three isolated beaches; Kitty Hawk, Kill Devil Hills and Nags Head. It was there that he happened upon the early morning testing conducted by the now famed Wright Brothers. Intrigued and mesmerised by the industry and dynamic Wills made his observations a daily pre-school routine and as the Wrights came closer to success Wills took the odd unofficial holiday from his lessons. He was rewarded one Thursday a few months later when he witnessed the world's first engine powered flight. Orville's first attempt was only 120 feet but Lipscomb knew that he was hooked for life.

Wills secured his pilot credentials just seven years later and at the opening of the Great War he volunteered for espionage duty operating mainly as a reconnaissance flyer for the Royal Flying Corps. His daring manoeuvres and close camera work provided still photographs that helped turn Western Front opportunity to advantage. When America entered the war in 1917 the now veteran and weary Lipscomb transferred allegiance to his homeland's uniform to both train and fight.

September 1918 and the carnage of Saint-Mihiel was scything fodder, no mercy spared for colour or creed; blood, mixed with noise and scream flowed in trench, tank and air. Wills Lipscomb knew that if he survived the day he would probably make it home to his beloved beaches. Having already downed two unfortunate enemy fighters Wills had no motivation left for his third sortie. During refuel he scanned the sky. Hundreds of young men pierced cloud, blast and thunder roar of battle. He witnessed another distant plane pummel toward the ground; its twisted frame recoiled against designed physic contorting it into a grotesque fireball. No marker would bear testimony to its charred remains.

Wills cast his mind back to 1903 and that December morning recalling the courage of the two Wright Brothers; two inventors of an ultimate good that men had hastily turned to evil. He held a warm coffee close to his cold lips and enjoyed the warmth in his bruised and calloused hands. Undeterred he walked back to his plane.

Boardroom Tennis

DETROIT, MICHIGAN – 1907

James has the same kind of brain as this young man.

The interview panel consisted of one company founder who sought a mechanical engineering team to produce his new automobile design. He encountered run of the mill candidates until one young man awoke him from his "bored-room" slumber. The question on crankshaft mechanics was aimed to garner understanding on potential capability but the response intrigued.

"Sorry sir, I'm not an engineer but I am a dreamer and I would like to become your company Joseph," the confident but not cocky interviewee responded and ventured forth, "for example, what is your greatest concern?" Fully awake the owner smiled and took the bait. "I am concerned that my competitors will steal my innovative car design. What do you suggest I do?" he parried. "Interesting question," was lobbed back, the owner taking it as surrender.... "If it was my design, I would paint the car black and test it during night darkness." The owner closed his notebook and he beckoned the young genius to continue.

"Your business surroundings suggest you want to remain a local manufacturer, but have you dreamed about becoming a national distributor?" the youngster offered. "We live in what will be the globe's biggest market and you should capitalise on that. Set up a national dealership network and to protect the integrity of your product your dealers should see it as a privilege to sell your automobiles but the pricing should be such that every family should see it as an absolute necessity to own one, maybe someday even two!" The owner interrupted... "What age are you son?" "I'm 21 sir, but my family say I have my grandfather's brain," the score levelled at 30:30 and before the owner could draw breath the youngster stole advantage. "Additionally sell replacement parts to each dealership and provide local mechanic training in each site. The everyday man will take this as your guarantee over their new purchase."

The owner sat amazed at the simplicity of the business model. "How can we afford all this?" he inquired of the grandfather's brain. "Easy sir," came the response and the awareness of the "we" inclusion. "At any one time this world is never too far away from war. Just set up a military division and secure transportation rights for all our armed services; there's police too and ambulance requirement." The game moved to the young man's advantage.

"Can you do all this?" the owner hesitated knowing that money was now on the table. "We can do it together sir," came a smart reply. "I'll do it all for only 20% of the annual turnover." The owner laughed not out of arrogance but at the sheer audacity of the bravery. "Well son that is a considerable amount of money for a fledgling company but I do like the way you think. We will have an abundance of set up costs and each penny will be required.......let me make a counter proposal. I will give you a 5% share of the company with a similar share of profit."

After a few moments the young man smiled. "Well sir, I wasn't even expecting to get in the door. You were kind to afford me the opportunity to express my dream and I reckon I'll accept your kind offer if you include an annual dividend payment too."

"If you are the company Joseph does that mean I am Pharaoh?" the owner smiled. "No sir. That means you are the boss but it also means that I will make you very rich!" the confident youth concluded.

Every family, business venture and community group requires a Joseph. The two grown men shook hands: game, set and match.

Shepherd Retreat

BADLANDS – NORTH DAKOTA 1911

**A bunch of sheep live in North Dakota; this is for my friend
Eamon the Shepherd.**

Through forest deep
and cut flower crag,
with stick in hand
and melted brow,
this shepherd's gaze
surveys his path,
this man is one with nature.

A narrow path
this man has beaten,
his mind fixed fast
his prey's heart beating,
a Stag he spies
on hillock turning,
this man is one with nature.

Oh Spirit deep
within me calling,
a world to wander
sights magnificent beholding,
this ticking clock
is in my grasp,
my being is one with nature.

The days gone past
are finished now
but my race is not yet over.
a new path I take
with foundation Rock,
I am still one,
I am nature.

One Fateful Morning

OVAL OFFICE, WASHINGTON D.C. – 6TH APRIL 1917

Not everyone likes D.C.
They make a lot of difficult impacting decisions there.

It was 5:30 a.m. and as usual Beth entered the Oval Office to make ready for the President's busy day. Her cleaning routine normally took 30 minutes.

"Oh no!" she cried, a single tear treading her face, "We are going to war."

A shuffle came from a long couch at the back of the famed room. "Good morning Beth," Mr. Wilson remarked. "What was that you said?"

"Oh Sir," Beth hesitated. "I can't help but notice that we are going to war."

"How in the dickens did you deduce that? I heard you open the door literally ten seconds ago," the slightly perplexed and amazed President responded.

"Sir.......I have cleaned this room for over 25 years! I know this room better than I do my own house and being the mother of two teenage sons I am also an expert at discernment!!" Beth laughed. "Look Sir....its easy! Firstly, your papers are laid out neatly across the long table but your glasses are across there, perched on the Presidential Desk. That means you have been thinking, pondering and walking the length of the room. Look! The carpet is brushed with your walking path and there are no other indentations elsewhere apart from over by the window where you have been standing and calculating." Beth's companion was startled and he beckoned her to continue. "There is no evidence of anybody else in the room because you and you alone had to make the decision. And if

I may say so Sir, I'm disappointed in you......I know you hate smoking but look," she said and pointed. "There are four fresh cigarette butts on the plate by the window. Not an ashtray...but a plate and that can only be you. Finding you here in yesterday's clothes suggests you have been awake all night tormented at the stark choice you have had to make. That I woke you Sir is the sign that you have made your decision."

"My oh my, Beth!" Woodrow Wilson exclaimed. "You are a regular Sherlock Holmes!"

"A who sir?" came Beth's sheepish response.

"A Sherlock Holmes, Beth. London's finest detective," the President continued.

"Indeed Beth, you are 100% correct in your deductions. I have wrestled with this decision for nearly three years and I cannot see any other way out of this global dilemma. Our European allies have lost millions of young men and our own Merchant Navy has been pummelled. Thirdly, funded by the coin of our foe, our southern borders will be antagonised by our very own neighbours and furthermore, pressure is being exerted by the Japanese from across the Pacific. Additionally the revolution in Russia has facilitated the movement of German troops from the eastern front to the west. We have to enter the war Beth and I do not like it...... You see I was elected on the premise that we would remain neutral but if such a conflict is to conclude it will require our nation, our armaments and our sacrifice to hasten and quicken an end play."

Beth decided to take a risk. She walked over to the President and gave him a short hug: like one given by a caring Grandmother. He acknowledged her encouragement and continued.

"Beth, in the coming days young men will be enamoured at the prospect of adventure. Alas many sons will fall to protect our freedoms: as in all historical record the price of liberty is blood. The grand scale of adventure will soon reduce itself to tough battlefield decisions and loss for our nation's parents. I bear this responsibility but that is what this job requires. I will cry with the mothers and share both the pride and anger of the fathers. I pray to Almighty God that the few will be required for the future of the many. I'll go now Beth and ready myself for the formalities. Thank you, Beth."

"Thank you Sir........and if I can add one more thing .....I believe it to be the right decision. Thank you for sharing with me." Beth concluded as she commenced another day in her familiar environment.

On Friday morning April 6, 1917, America formally entered World War One.

Forgotten Lives

MILWAUKEE, WISCONSIN - 1921

You never know what people have been through.

Having returned home from military service at the age of 24, Bill Miller felt he was too young to be called a veteran. He found it difficult to settle back to old routines and familiar faces. People could not imagine his wartime experiences, particularly the recurring sleeping hour nightmares. Most nights these recoiling repulsive horrors revisited Bill placing him once more in the mud and rat-infested soaking drench of Northern France.

Leaving his fortifications Bill would stagger across the ghostly silhouette of no man's land, through the never-ending bombardment and bullet hail. Anxious enemy machine gunners sliced the beaten land mowing the approaching attack shadow by shadow. Though still asleep Bill could smell the pungent fumes of gas and death. All around fell until he alone would plough into the offending trench with rifle and bayonet to cut and slash human frailty; each pale fearful face etched and seared forever upon his memory.

Job hunting was hard as returning heroes competed for limited opportunity. Bill had a fortuitous meeting with one of his father's friends who offered him an opening at his burgeoning motorcycle factory; one of the few manufacturers that survived the war. Bill enjoyed his work as a metal fabricator. He especially loved the bikes, committing to save a portion of his weekly earnings in an effort to buy one. Each piece he felt was a work of art. Metal, paint and chrome combining with liquid to form a perfect moving unit; the purchaser having a whole continent to explore. Unhindered freedom on wheels.

One evening a fire took hold in the factory's furnace hall and all the employees rushed out in frightened frenzy. Bill rushed in unprotected, extinguishing the threat while saving two lives in the process. The owners offered Bill his coveted prize as a reward but Bill hesitated. He explained that he had seen how rewards had worked in the military; the initial rejoicing would soon be replaced by the jealousy and bitterness of his co-workers and friends. He explained that he would continue to save but he negotiated a commitment from the owners to invest in a rehabilitation fund for veterans. They agreed seeing the advantage from both a philanthropic and marketing perspective; many of the psychologically damaged men were proud and loving owners of their heritage product.

A generation of Milwaukeeans benefited from the fund's benevolence albeit Bill's nightmares continued though at a reduced rate. He still saw the carnage of the trench and heard the screams and roars for girlfriend, wife and mother. As he grew older the bodies still fell but these nights the fallen bore the image of Bill's own face.

Millie Nelson

NEW HAMPSHIRE - 1922

Nature is startlingly beautiful but each person is more unique.

Millie Nelson was birthed into Fall beauty
on a colourful tree lined farm.
The tar brushed creosote fence stood
in contrast to the shifting hues of autumn;
bright rich red, yellows, artisan greens, browns and sunburst orange.
As a child Millie Nelson learnt about the forest
it's mysterious ways and haunting frame.
Millie Nelson decided that she would stay in her birth State
until The Lord called her home.

Millie Nelson played in the midst of the local forests
and she knew her Fall friends by native name;
Whisper, Swinging Leaf, Melody,
Old Cringe Bark, Hollow Hole and Briar Scratch.
Millie Nelson grew and marked each Fall,
capturing a grainy black and white then later in color;
her photos as distinctive as Monet's poppy
or a patina explosion of Van Gogh's exquisite oils.

Millie Nelson knew the rural cut-through roads,
the spanning red painted bridges covered by wooden umbrellas
hand hewn by folks of ago.
Millie Nelson delighted in the wispy mingle of dewy morn mist
that faded and danced with the industry of scented woodstove smoke.
Millie Nelson married a neigboring farmer,
they loved each other until her untimely demise at the age of 38.
The earth called her home,
the hand of time claiming promise.

The forest heaved, creaked and moaned,
her named friends agreed to commemorate with solemn blaze.
They burst forth into a celebration of kaleidoscopic magnificence,
never before seen, Heaven sent, colors,
added to the usual beauty of born leaf, tall bark and rejoicing branch.
Millie Nelson smiled once more,
her spirit released to drift home.

Sleight of Hand

LUBEC, MAINE – 1928

Maine is a good place to enjoy a walk. Careful though, don't wander too far.

The five FBI cars left Lubec early September after another uneventful summer; their third annual attempt to unravel the source of illegal Canadian Whisky smuggling besetting the entire prohibition suffering nation. They had arrived the previous May and merged into the daily lives of what they thought were unsuspecting Lubecians. They had observed and investigated the daily routine: the fishing, the burgeoning summer tourist trail from northern cities, the seasonal fruit pickers and the town's commercial life. They left empty handed for the warmer southern winter confused and perplexed, albeit with better tans.

Allowing two further weeks of normal life in motion and fearful of an additional surprise federal visit the beginning of October heralded the re-instigation of the "Burchett Plan" the daring enterprise involving all Lubec but conceived in 1921 by the civic minded public representative Dempsey Burchett.

A team of builders descended upon the town's southern industry zone and dismantled a wooden carcass covered cluster of main road buildings to reveal Lubec's false "official" Canadian Border Crossing. Canadian flags were hoisted and the Stars and Stripes were carefully stored for the following April. Burchett deployed uniformed border guards and documentation personnel where unsuspecting visitors would be "processed." Welcome to Canada signage was erected and another team went about town dismantling tell-tale hints together with replacing all vehicle licence plates. America was now unofficially officially Canada! Even if the FBI did an unseasonal winter check they would do so with local agents who were in Burchett's pockets. Agents from further afield would and could not legally cross an international border.

On the northern side fishing warehouses became alcohol holding centres and the trawlers became the smuggler's valuable tools. Tonnage was growing every year across the short north Atlantic run from Canada and the money flowed on tap. Come December the sheltered waters of Johnson Bay would freeze and literally thousands of cases of cheap and expensive Canadian Whisky would be dispensed geographically by dog pulled sleigh across the frozen ice. The small shore towns became the gateway to Detroit, Chicago and beyond. Burchett's web extended as far as the unquenchable thirst of California. Burchett had in effect left the FBI impotently stumped. Civic Dempsey's new wealth was heavily invested in Lubec; the whole town and every family prospered.

In April the process was reversed and Lubec became American again. Flush with cash the residents relished the break to welcome the new tourist season warmly. The fishermen fished, the hotelier's hotelled, the mechanics mechaniced, the children played and the FBI arrived to build back their tans. Some of the agents became champion fishermen, some even retired there.

"Someday this will be destroyed. They'll build a bridge across to Canada and make all this official but until then let us all enjoy the fruits of our labor and when prohibition ends well....well we'll just play with exchange rates and keep our rustling going," remarked Dempsey Burchett at an unminuted council meeting in 1931.

As prophesised the Franklin Delano Roosevelt connecting bridge between America and Canada was opened in 1962. Dempsey Burchett became a retiree fisherman with several well tanned retired FBI friends.

Cheers!

Good Fortune in Hungry Country

ARKANSAS – 1929

Down with angry men.

The card game had been rudely interrupted by the Sherriff. Twenty minutes later the engine of the 1924 Ford Ton Truck idled outside the courthouse; the angry card-playing driver impatiently awaited the parolee who a short time later exited and sauntered across to the ride.

"So you're going to be working at the Wilkes farm," the driver ventured to his stoic and silent passenger. "You're fortunate: though for a young man Wilkes sure has a lifetime of meanness in him. Folks roundabouts say that Wilkes imported half his meanness cause there wasn't enough here! Way too much meanness for one man and he's cruel too. He had his self a beautiful wife and sons but his cruelness didn't endear and they ups and left. Wilkes sits on the porch most days now, moanin, drinkin and cussin......ya mean and cruel."

The passenger shifted; a nasty spirit resting uncomfortably in the cabin.

"Though Wilkes isn't as bad as the next farm up," continued the driver. "That guy is twice as mean and cruel as Wilkes......and twice as ugly too: shot the last two parolees for no reason. Just upped and shot them. Ya, you caught yourself a fortunate break getting the Wilkes place. Least you'll get half a Sabbath off at Wilkes; a prisoner, even one released, is only half a man. Yes sir; you caught yourself a fortunate break. Ah look! I'll drop you at the gate as my card game beckons my return; it's only a two mile walk and it looks like you'll beat the storm. There ya go and good luck mister; you sure is lucky getting the Wilkes."

The fortunate passenger disembarked and surveyed his new surroundings. He stood silently and smelt the surging heaviness of the day; a charge of heat and electricity permeating the dusty air. The sky was darkening by the minute; hues of deep purple, misty bruised yellow and grey heaved toward the well-worn pathway. The raging tornado commenced his walk toward the distant buildings, his thoughts fermenting with each step. "Reckon I'll show this Wilkes what meanness is and I'll extract some vengeance for his wife and sons; he's not even half a man who treats his kin suchlike. Depending how I feel I'll continue beyond to his neighbour and seek justice for those he shot.....though depending on that looming storm I might have to leave that until tomorrow. Ya....driver was right! I'm sure fortunate to be getting the Wilkes farm."

Revival

OSBORNE, KANSAS - 1931

Fraudsters operate in all walks of life; take your time trusting.

The chauffeured Chrysler Imperial pulled up and released health, wealth and prosperity preacher Jedediah Thorngood who entered the back of the large tent.

"Gene, are you here?" Thorngood's brusk discourteous voice demanded of his assistant who appeared from the other side of the canopy. "Everything done Gene? Seats, car-park laid out, volunteers recruited, and most importantly donation baskets at the ready?" Thorngood inquired, Gene nodding in the affirmative. "How many here Gene? I need a good night," the preacher added.

"Everything is set Reverend: about 800 here already," reported his loyal assistant of four years.

"Give it another 15 minutes Gene. Its six weeks until harvest and these people will be praying for a bumper crop. I'll try to draw it toward the thousand capacity; it should be a $2,000 night," Thorngood spoke almost only to himself.

Half an hour later Jedediah Thorngood ventured to his pulpit and the rousing applause of his adorning congregation. He soaked up the adulation. "Howdy folks, I'm Jedediah Thorngood, yawl can call me Reverend."

Gene stood behind the veiled curtain, a frown etched on his weary face. "Look at that," he muttered "he forgot his Bible again."

Settling the crowd and bowing to pray Jedediah noticed the lack of Bible. "Doesn't matter," he thought "the only book I need is my ledger."

Without Bible or a solitary scriptural context or verse Jedediah launched forth delivering the heat drenched audience into a frenzy of expectation. He evoked blessing for the forthcoming harvest and mixed his talk with a collection of home spun farm tales. The few discerning left but the majority sat bestowing rapt delirious attention: their second coming had arrived.

Behind the scene Gene watched, disgust sweeping through his slight frame. "This man was not aptly named," he mused, the convictions of the last few months quickening his spirit. "This man is not a man of God. He's a fraudster, a charlatan, a manipulator of extreme proportion, a legalised gangster defrauding the gullible. Why he's nothing but a hypocrite like the Pharisee of old. Look at him there with his beguiling smile flashing his pearly white teeth."

Gene had been reading his Bible and was assured that "The Reverend" was contorting the truth into his own image. "Surely the aim of preaching was to convey truth, encourage examination of sin to foster repentance," Gene thought, his conviction growing with every night. "Tonight I even had to tell him where we are!! He should be living a life of service to God's will. People need to hear of free grace onto salvation, mercy, forgiveness and Christ's Blood, not this contrived emotional garbage."

Gene picked up Thorngood's Bible which fell open in Revelation Chapter 18. "Come out of her, my people, lest you share in her sins and lest you receive of her plagues," screamed from the page searing Gene's conscience. Gene settled his mind and senses, packed his meagre belongs and left to follow his new Master. He walked to the roadside, stuck out his thumb and soon secured passage to the next town.

On stage Jedediah Thorngood revelled in the adoration. He was pleased with his delivery and performance; one of his best he felt; one to be remembered. Thorngood looked across the room and smiled as the volunteer's collected the baskets. "Yes indeed," he thought, "it might even be a $3,000 night."

A Road is Never Black

KEY WEST – FLORIDA 1932

Distant mountains are never green,
they are purple and a road is never black.

They say you should never meet a hero. I do not subscribe to that fallacy. In hindsight he was more of a friend.

Every summer I would holiday with my Grandfather and each day after our walk we would stop at Sloppy Joe's: Gramps for a cool refreshing beer and I would enjoy a popsicle or a soda. He was there most days; sometimes in the middle of all things entertaining the crowd. At other times he was alone, irked by the company, the attention or some other internal dynamic known only to himself. It was during one of those morose occasions that I approached him.

"You know Mister," I declared, "I too would like to be a pen ponderer!" He laughed, his solemn pensiveness immediately lifting and our bond was forged.

I returned again the following summer as an angst wrought teenager. There he was and our quick reconnection followed. I tended to his lawns that summer and he helped Gramps paint our homestead fence. I told him that I had read one of his books and I asked him how he did it.

"I'm less of a writer," he replied. "I'm more of an expander. Once you understand that it becomes easier." He continued ......

"For example, a road is never just black.
A road is full of transient life and colour as well as being a means of vehicular conveyance. A road is about the trucking man who singularly

roams the tentacles of our vast landscape collecting stories and memories.
A road is the pathway to adventure and opportunity;
the paving stone of industry and endeavour.
A road is never black.

Similarly the truth is never simply the truth.
The truth is a complexity.
To the Police it is about establishment of fact and discernment.
The truth always possesses shading and varying degrees of insight.
It is obtuse; angular,
a double edged sword.

Likewise love is hardly ever love.
It can be covetous perhaps even lustful.
Love is complicated but it is sometimes found,
it then becoming a battle to retain.
It can hurt, bruise and lose its glow;
it is the most tender and fragile of things.
True love serves, often at personal cost
and it is hardly ever reciprocated.

You see, a story carries words but it is mostly about expansion.
A man once proclaimed of me that I was merely a writer.
I corrected him stating categorically that I was a builder."

"Wow!!" I just asked a simple question. He laughed with Gramps.

"Though when all is said and done," he added as he ruffled my hair, "a
smile will always please."

I spent the following seven summers there before the war called me. I
served in Europe and upon my return I trained in medicine.

I was deeply saddened upon the news of his death. The world mourned
the passing of a literary giant; I however had lost both my friend and a

significant portion of my childhood. I smile frequently as I contemplate my good fortune at having known two such fine gentlemen.

To me he was Mr. H or Hemm, but mostly a casual "Hi" sufficed. From his side I was always called "Ponder."

Bloodlines

LIVINGSTON, KENTUCKY - 1932

Fortunate are those whose hobbies become their work and legacy.

I drove down the Lexington to Livingston road at a gentle pace; window down, the cool of the evening penetrating and refreshing the cabin. I pulled up at the old house which nestled in the cultivations of Daniel Boone country where she greeting me warmly with an embrace she saved for only a few. She showed me my room where I restlessly slept in expectation of my early morning call.

After our hearty breakfast we walked down the red soiled sand packed path to the stable, she reminding me that all this is in our blood. She reminded me that there is a business side to all endeavours, the buying and selling, provision of comfortable shelter and food, electricity and water demands etc. I smiled; she knew she was repeating herself though she added that for some it was 95% business and only 5% joy. She subscribed to the latter; she blessed to be able to devote almost complete dedication to her lifestyle.

We stood watching the young jockeys parade the early morning runners. The landscape bore a misty hue, shards of weak light casting their early morning vagueness. Carefully tended fences proudly displayed the overnight built glinting spider-webs and the sounds of waking yawning life came from not too distant branch and earth bore burrow. As the sun grew it drained the last vestiges of dewy moisture depositing the perfect condition upon our day.

The proud, yet not haughty, horses started with a canter; spirited demeanours reined in expertly which the riders slowly built with mounting strength. We stood and watched this cavalry charge to finish line: raw, unhinged power unleashed to almost furious pace. To observe is to see time stand still. The pounding echoes drew nearer and on passing we could hear the flared nostril breathing. Singular beasts orchestrated to magnificent co-ordinated union. A cold collar sweat tingle of excitement was left in the wake.

I looked at her; she initially unaware, but upon her turning to see my reaction she instead caught my devoted smile. We had often times shared this unadulterated pleasure calling it the pinnacle of human existence: no false motivations, no self-interest, just a sharing of our fondest pursuit midst the love we had for each other.

That afternoon I said goodbye to my Grandmother and promised a soon return. She again reminded me that one day this would all be mine. I suppose in some way she wanted to ensure herself that we shared the same devotion and dedication.

Bluegrass Friday

APPALACHIAN COUNTRY LANE – WEST VIRGINIA 1940

If you are driving somewhere new turn up a hidden country lane.

Every Friday
neon light,
hum and crackle
humid night.

MC standing
dance floor hall,
building the tension
announcing the call.
Sweat pour face
voice all a roar,
long night ahead
Oh what a chore.

Baccy chew
then baccy spit
guys outside
girls inside, sit.
Band arrives
strings and beats
music roll
soon hits the feet.

Banjo thumping
4-4 beat
clashing cymbals
guitar streak,
bass line tango
fiddle pick
singer wailing
like a conjurer's trick.
Quick pace fusion
rag time roll
feet now stomping
warming from cold.

Beer bar heaving
bottles in hand
restlessness quickening
the week's last stand.
Swaying rhythm
rolling crowd
Life in tizzy
Music loud.

One last dance
revellers moan,
Friday night magic
hangover groan.
Cars they a leaving
stories all told,
Bluegrass rhythm
is the poor man's gold.

My Missing

PEARL HARBOUR, HAWAII, DECEMBER 8, 1941

For those we miss.

Till we meet again.
Till autumn's leaf births forth her golden splendour.
Till the night watch ceases and day heralds a harvest bounty.
Till sleeps dream cascades to a hidden living beauty.
All is mystery
Till we meet again.

Till we smile again.
Till child's laugh breathes a merriment cure to all around her.
Till a joyous heart sings praise to worship its mighty Creator.
Till tears that flow fast collect to memories brighter.
All rest now
Till we smile again.

Till we love again,
Till we sit and hope with hearts that can beat no faster.
Till we talk and plot with all futures gaze a flutter.
Till we stoop and break with eyes that can look no deeper.
All distance gone
We shall indeed love again.

Steeltown Mothers

BETHLEHEM, PENNSYLVANIA 1943

The old steel mills are a sorry sight but they have an incredible history.

For a while we were the captains of industry,
rulers of the realm for a time.
We worked and crafted our implements of victory,
the nemesis of our enemy; their pounding destruction.

Steel mills and furnace forge
hot fire flame,
white heat moulding
tank, ship and plane.
Our goal was fuelled by Appalachian coal,
we built our hope in this Bethlehem home,
each piece to be aimed at skin and bone.

We despised the sons of our foe
yet we pitied their mothers:
they buried their dead
we knew ours by name.
When one fell we embraced the heartbroken
held our nerve and applied all the more vigour,
love for ours our chief emotion,
obedience and love racking carnage nightly upon our souls.

When our men returned we applied ourselves again,
some to kitchen and some to depression.
We fortified ourselves once more
to raise the next generation for war.

We were the captains of industry for a while
and only too soon we will be again.

12 Weeks till Tomorrow

TUPELO - MISSISSIPPI 1947

Make up your own music for this one.

The young boy ran into a room full of visitors, "Hey folks!" he smiled grabbing everyone's attention. "Would you like me to sing for you?" He proceeded to sing in a low rich voice while swinging to his rhythm's beat.

It seems like 12 weeks since Friday
since I danced all night with you,
It seems like 12 weeks since Saturday
since we walked this road; us two,
It seems like 12 weeks since Sunday
since I lay beside your smile,
It seems like 12 weeks since Monday
since I dreamed, your hand in mine.

I hope its 12 weeks till tomorrow
so we can start all over tonight
and if its 12 weeks till tomorrow
then spend that time with me.

It feels like 12 weeks since Tuesday
since I kissed you slow last night,
It feels like 12 weeks since Wednesday
since we fought with all our might,
It feels like 12 weeks since Thursday
making up can be so much fun,
then its back once more to Friday
and you're still the only one.

And if its 12 weeks till tomorrow
then spend that time with me
lets put the effort in now honey
thats the working week for me.

The boy's parents cheered and clapped for the young blues prodigy but inwardly every other adult wondered how a twelve year old could know so much. The normally stony faced, prim and proper visitors all smiled at each other in acknowledgement, but they remained thin-lipped and vacantly silent. The young boy ran back outside to continue playing with his cousins.

Anyone for Desert?

INDIANAPOLIS, INDIANA – 1951

My folks were once the only guests in a restaurant full of plotting mafia.

Hand in hand, smiling honeymooners Hank and Ellen Bateman entered the hotel's restaurant. Apart from an elderly couple, the husband of same on the phone, the grand room was empty. On requesting a table the waiter looked to the old man who nodded approval: the Batemans sat to study the menu. Ellen, facing the old man observed him nodding throughout the phone conversation he finally saying "yes" then hanging up he returned attention back to his aged wife.

"They look like a lovely old couple Hank," Ellen remarked. "They must be nearly 90; probably married for over sixty years. Are you listening Hank?"

"Sorry Hun, just trying to decide between steak and fish. What did you say?" replied Hank busy weighing his options.

"Probably married over 60 years, the old couple over there. Imagine being married over 60 years Hank! That means they got married in the last century," repeated Ellen, while Hank remained lost in his own thought.

The phone rang again and the old man answered. He nodded again to himself, said "yes" and returned once more to his wife.

"Whats that about 60 years Hun?" inquired Hank, his decision finally made. Ellen repeated the earlier observation. "Wow! Fancy that," continued Hank. "I'd like to think we'll make that Ellen; who knows, maybe even more." Ellen gazed into her new husband's eyes and blushed."

Entree and dinner arrived and the wine and conversation flowed. The phone rang again and the old man nodded once more before answering his usual affirmative. Soft music played in the background; both couples enjoyed the atmosphere. The phone rang again and another "yes" was provided.

"They're getting ready to leave Hank.....the old couple. They look so sweet and he looks so kind and gentle helping her with her coat and everything. She sure is fortunate having a husband like him, though I'm luckier Hank," Ellen said as she reached across to hold her husband's hand. Hank smiled, he knew what he wanted for desert and it wasn't on the menu!

The old man stood up slowly and balanced against his table. With the aid of a stick he alone walked toward Hank and Ellen's table. Ellen saw him approach and smiled confident that he was going to pass on his congratulations. He smiled benevolently as he leaned over to speak.

"Hank and Ellen Bateman! Only ye is on yer honeymoon I'd have ye both killed like those I've just despatched with those phonecalls, ya hear me?" the smiling man whispered to the now stunned couple. "If ye breathe a word or tell anyones what me or my wife looks like yer lives won't be worth livin." Pointing to Ellen he continued, "I'll start with you. I'll have ya skinned alive and I'll feed ya to the hogs, ya hearin me missus and as for you," he turning to Hank "you'll just wish that Genghis Khan was left loose in yer stomach with an itchin sword."

The old man went back for his wife and as they exited he turned back and got Hank's attention..... "and as for you son, if ya want yer marriage to last ya better start listening to yer gorgeous wife." Hank lost his appetite.

The smiling waiter approached and cleared the table.

"Who.......who was that?" stumbled a very nervous Hank as Ellen tried to mask her red eyes.

"You don't want to know Sir. Believe me you don't want to know," the waiter replied.

"But they looked so happy," stuttered Ellen.

"Ya," responded the waiter. "Amazing couple; they probably have one of the happiest marriages around these here parts, over 60 years you know......anyone for desert?"

Pension Plan at Lyles

MEMPHIS, TENNESSEE 1967

Retired at 36! What you would do?

The post war Jake Tandy was a tough man and an even harder father.
He cared for future provision but in the process he never enjoyed
the raising of his four children: they a chore not a blessing.
A college education, Jake felt, would equip with the skill-set to provide
but that drive was directed without an ounce of heartfelt love.
"Its a tough world out there and those sumsobeaches better get real,"
Jake would say over and over and over again.
It was therefore much to his chagrin when his 18 year old boy Lyle
decided to open a cafe beside the new music studios in 1950.

Jeanie, Lyle's girlfriend and soon to be wife, carried "Assistant Technician"
as her important job description in the new music studio.
Over the following years she completed a host of tasks
from recording duties to hospitality where she befriended many of the guests.
Despite the continual moaning of her future father in law, Jeanie and Lyle
constituted a formidable partnership, they together devising a clever plan:
musical legends would record and next door they would eat.
Jeanie would tell Lyle who was in town he would buy their respective
recordings which the guests would later autograph at the popular cafe.
Everything from spinning 45s to LPs and guitars to snare drums
were signed; included in which were numerous movie posters
inscribed by the silver screen visitors of the "Million Dollar Quartet."
Time moved on and in 1959, Lyle and Jeanie Tandy moved to
a larger premises, again next door to a now larger and more famous studio.
Jeanie and Lyle continued hosting and feeding until the studio closed.

"So you're finished. 36 and kaput! Told ya..." Jake remonstrated soon after.
"Just startin Pops," Lyle responded with a smile.
Opening a basement vault Lyle revealed thousands of autographed items:
literally the world's largest collection of pristine celebrity memorabilia.
Jeanie and Lyle sold every last piece and invested their prize in
not two but three apartment complexes all paying a handsome monthly rental.
They cared for and nursed a later thankful Jake and they started to
invest in community welfare projects. Their love over years assisted thousands.
Dads, encourage your children and their respective endeavours.
Be thankful; one day it will be returned.

Any News is Good News

ST. LOUIS, MISSOURI – 25 MAY 1968

One day I will visit the Gateway Arch.....might even fly through it.

Inauguration Day had arrived for St. Louis' Gateway Arch. The visitor's centre of the impressive 630ft monument was approaching its first birthday and a huge crowd was expected to observe the official opening by Vice President Hubert Humphrey. City officials were confident that the Arch would capture the public's imagination; they hopeful of future tourist spend. Fearful of a prank the Mayor had taken security precautions and every airport with a 50 mile radius of the Arch was closed and secured by police and military. Nothing would be left to chance: the city needed publicity and employment. Unfortunately rain materialised and while the expected crowds did not arrive the press did. Rolling cameras would ensure the required nationwide exposure.

Norman and Lynne Parker were modern day adventurers. Both in their early 30s they had travelled the world during the previous decade and had undertaken some amazing exploits: they boasted a camel ride across the Moroccan Sahara, the eluding of arrest in Jakarta and sailing from Sydney to New Zealand as their highlights. Today's plan would garnish global notoriety but their identities would have to remain secret.

Inauguration hour had arrived and the adrenaline rush was palpable. Party politics had been suspended for the day as dignitaries met and greeted while securing valuable photo opportunities with the White House official. The collective mood was high as the approaching bi-plane of old was heard and seen from the Arch's view-deck. The joyous mood slackened as Parker lowered his approach toward the Arch. The perplexed Mayor did well to hide his fury as he looked anxiously at both the plane and the famous visitor. Flashbulb lights penetrated the foreboding grey sky and the TV crews, while staggered at Parker's audacity, captured the moment as the bi-plane swept underneath the Arch while looping back under again to return south in the direction of the Mississippi. Vice President Humphrey was intrigued, a wry smile hidden behind his veiled hands. Silence permeated the official platform while city officials quickly assured that the perpetrator would be caught at a neighbouring airport.

Norman Parker charted the 35 miles south to the outskirts of Festus where he parachuted onto the back of Lynne's waiting motorbike. The plane jettisoned into the Mississippi which, given the rainfall, was flowing in full spate. The authorities were at a complete loss as to their identities.

Vice President Humphreys was rushed by helicopter to his awaiting plane. The rain fell heavily and casual observers saw a small number of dark shadows embark and depart. The Air force escort jet also set off, a second passenger visible in the rear. The specially adapted F-100 flew north, first sinking low to skirt under Missouri's Arch. Later that evening the two planes arrived at Andrews Airforce Base. Evidence of Humphrey's excursion never emerged, although St. Louis' Mayor had his suspicions.

Exploits at the Gateway Arch captured public and media attention across the globe. The city offered a never claimed reward for information leading to the identification of the culprits. The Parker's left Missouri, their coffers further enhanced by a front company cheque which would ensure sufficient funds for another five years travel activity. They never returned to St. Louis.

The tourists arrived and the string-puller smiled; the city would receive the promised lease of life. "Any news is good news," he reflected; his investment had garnished the much sought after publicity to ensure intrigue and mystery for a long long time.

Question Time

WAPAKONETA, OHIO – OCTOBER 1969

Be an individual.

There's always one kid, one in every town: actually look closer there is always one on every street, each classroom, school bus, team, boat load, car load and mother lode. What is it? ....a kid that doesn't fit in! Kincaid Brubaker was that kid in Wapakoneta, Ohio: suppose he was singled out by his name, Kincaid Brubaker. Like who would do that to a kid?

A solitary kind of 15 year old, Kincaid had a fine list of awkward achievements. He was the kid that read at gym class, the kid who ran the wrong way at football, the kid that held the baseball bat upside down and inside out. He was the kid that other kids were afraid of being seen beside. Yes; a solitary kind of 15 year old.

The annual "Question Time" event arrived at school; you know...... some of the teachers together with the principal would sit on stage and answer the deep philosophical questions of hormone raging teenagers. A day universally hated by teachers given some of the personal observations they would be asked about. Sometimes a day loved by pupils who regularly fought for the "who can best embarrass a teacher moment" prize. After the usual insipid, dull and boring questions, some of which were obvious plants, Kincaid took the microphone.

"Earlier this summer," he commenced "a man walked on the moon." The class took a collective breath, what was this donk going to ask? "Well," continued Kincade "I was thinking to myself what does a man do after walking on the moon? You know, won't everything he does after that just simply bore? Like.....em....what can possibly ever challenge him after that......like what could ever beat that?" The staged panel were discombobulated, even the principle couldn't answer. "I'll ring the Mayor," he offered. Class continued.......

The Principal rang the Mayor who couldn't answer he in turn rang the Senator who passed the question to the State Governor. The Governor pondered and perplexed he rang the President who again couldn't discern an adequate answer. A few weeks later the Principle interrupted Kincaid's class, "Excuse me Miss Perdue," he apologised "but the President is on the phone for Kincaid." The class gasped, the teacher fainted.

Twenty minutes later Kincaid and the Principal returned, Kincaid's new friends surrounded him. "Well buddy, what happened, did you get your answer?" the quarterback inquired while the head cheerleader snuggled close to the new celebrity.

Kincaid bit his lip, drawing everyone even closer. "He said I should work in computers and I told him that would be too easy. Just a bunch of 1's and 0's which I outgrew when I was three. He said I'd go a long way and he asked me what I'd like to do and that he would help me with whatever endeavour I wished to choose."

"That was nice of him," the eye batting cheer leader purred.

"Ya, I suppose it was," agreed Kincaid now nestling closer. "I told him that I would like to be President but that I'd do things differently to him. Told him that if I was the leader of a country that had the capability to send a man to the moon that I would talk to my enemies rather than blow the absolute smithereens out of them." Miss Purdue fainted a second time.

"And.........what did he say to that?" the Principle said in awe of the young man.

"He hung up!" answered Kincaid. "Reckon I'd expect that of an eleven year old," mused the centre of attention "but not of a fully grown fool."

Life in Wapakoneta went back to normal. Kincaid was asked back to football and baseball and the following week at gym class fifteen kids were found to be reading, including the quarterback.

Seven Words on State Street

MONTPELIER, VERMONT – 10TH JULY 1974

Dream BIG dreams. Then work hard toward their fruition.

The shark fin chromed tail of a shining black '59 Buick Electra
slowed and stopped outside the General Post Office.
Fourteen year old Zac Zmudzinski, ZZ to his friends, was idling;
waiting rather impatiently for his mother.
"Hey Kid!" came the shout from the cruiser.
"Highway?" with raised hands indicating that the driver was lost.
A wide eyed and open mouthed ZZ pointed west.
"Whatya doin here Mister? Nuttin ever happens in Vermont!" ZZ stammered.
"Just driving. Thanks Buddy," at which the Electra glided off.

Nobody, including his mother, believed that Zac had met Elvis and
he just driving on a short break between tours.
That encounter changed Zac's life.
He bought a guitar, added a middle C and became Zacc Ski.

"SKI," the band started slow.
They wrote a bunch of songs, toured small gigs, mostly schools and halls
and in 1978 they got their first air-time and played the State Fair.
Graduating beyond State lines SKI grew nationally then yonder abroad.
TV, Magazines and Radio followed
and city by city the fans came.
Zacc told his story at every show and slowly people believed;
even his mother!
Six Grammy's later Zacc's only regret is that
Elvis will never enjoy one of his songs.

Every July Zacc Ski returns to the Montpelier Post Office.
He stands in the same place and pays homage to his two heroes;
Elvis and more importantly his mother who passed in 2011.
As Zacc now knows, big things can happen.......even in Vermont.

Hope

NORTH CHIHUAHUAN DESERT, NEW MEXICO – 1981

Find your Hope and hold on..........tight

After an arduous three week journey and furtive border crossing the surviving Diaspora of thirty illegal Mexicans were herded like cattle onto a non-descript plain coloured bus. Armed guards sat front and back securing their chattel; they driven to extreme, not by opportunity, but by desperation. Hated by their captors the ragged entourage were regarded as valueless in their humanity but priceless as a future income stream.

He sat back into the plastic seat trying to mentally process the last month. He had paid an extortionate escape fee but was told that morning that he would not be "awarded freedom" for another three years. His labour would be sub-contracted to handlers and in exchange a deduction would be taken from discounted earnings: 90% the first year, 80% the second and 60% the third. Even then he wondered if they would keep their word.

The bus drove into approaching desert country. An arid treeless stretch of volcanic abyss opened up together with its sandstone scorch of hot dry bone dune. They were given a thirty minute comfort break and as he stood out of the bus he looked toward a scratchy blue sky mixed with a hint of red and haze; he gazed further toward a distant mirage of purple shimmer.

Small groups huddled to smoke and except for the disenfranchised cursing and murmurings of his fellow passengers it was silent. He separated himself from the group to inhale the scene. He spotted the ancient slow burn trails and imagined the pathless meanderings of the hunting gather man of old. He contemplated those who slept in the shady shadowed crevices beneath the flat top mesas and steepled buttes. Skyward rock pillars imposed an imprisoning barrier of dehydrated rock; walls shaped by windblown time. He was mesmerised by the landscape, the prickled cactus and scalp brush bush. He smiled as he digested nature's bountiful reserve.

Before they re-embarked upon their journey he glanced across the desert's protruding sweep and back toward the horizon. Most people, he thought, never experienced such freedom. He was thankful that he had tasted it for twenty minutes: the prospect of return became his hope.

Reminiscences of a Hollywood Hellraiser

L.A. - CALIFORNIA 1984

These guys were the early cinema heroes.

"You ask me what it was like?" and with an ostentatious wave
and a theatrical flourish of his hand he continued,
"It was marvellous......absolutely marvellous."

"Can I describe it? ......em.
Well it was like the sharp retort of a snare drum.
Yes...a snare drum; you know, a rapid staccato paradiddle
building frantically to its climatic end. Slightly unhinged I suppose.

Nightlife town, dancehall sway,
cocktail hour, time to play.
Ritz, glitz, all that fashion,
lipstick red, prowler's passion.
Rum numb brain, nicotine haze,
wired insane, latest craze.
Fetching stare, tango eyes,
hips with rhythm, blood filled highs.
Press is out, flashbulb fury,
backlash splash, another story.
Back on set, name in lights,
out again,
loved those nights."

"How did I do it you ask?
Simple really.
I endeavoured with best attempt, to keep my name in the newspapers."

"And would I do it again? ....Would we do it again?"
"Yes, I would," and with steely resolve
and a last faint glimmer of flamboyant daring he concluded,
"There are only a few of us left now you know,
so yes we would; we bloody well would........and more!"

Its My Turn Now

AUGUSTA, GEORGIA – 1990

Peach trees, golden leaves.....heres to Georgia nights out.

There is a small carefully painted black gate down by a trail bend on land that was once farmed by the Hyker boy's father. On this rarely used farm road almost everything smells of the past; even the grass, it feels, is rusted over and a few remaining scraggy peach tree branches stretch with dignified poise into the unbroken sky. The younger brother, David, continues to make the half mile walk to the old family gated plot and has done so most evenings since they buried his older brother twenty years ago. David sits mostly by his brother's headstone and remembers. "Don't worry David, I'll look after you," the older boy quoted hundreds of times. "Don't worry, I'll look after you." David can still reach into his past and hear the love and care etched in his brother's voice.

Often the memories bring a smile like when David thought his father caught him smoking his first cigarette and he confided to his brother's sensibilities. Again the time he snuck out and borrowed or depending on how you look at it "stole" the Archer's car so he could visit Laura. Their first drinking session with friends down by the river; David drank so much beer that night he vowed he'd never drink again: that promise was soon broken! The strongly forged tag team bond and their antics continued at football, baseball, with visits to the lights of Augusta and with the feigning of elaborate James Brown moves while steamed in a Waffle House at 2am. David always found trouble and even the odd arrest didn't deter his brother from promising firstborn allegiance to that universal law: "Don't worry, I'll look after you."

In 1969 David was drafted and true to his word his older sibling volunteered. Vietnam heralded a wasted clarion call and battle madness ensued. Though used to the balmy Georgia air the boys found the jungle insufferable. The insects, fevers, monsoon rains and shearing scalding red hot bullets took toll. Friends fell and during one dark night-watch a sniper scored on the elder Hyker. David was holding his brother's hand when he passed. "Who'll look after you now David?" were his last words; David's response, "Don't worry, it's my turn now," the last words heard. True to his word David took over the farm and cared for his family. One day soon he will rest alongside his much loved friend.

There is a lot of love in this life. There is a lot of pain in this life too. Equally, there is a lot of love in the midst of never ending pain.

Learn to Scream

RHODE ISLAND 1999

If you are going to scream about something make sure it is something important.

Jane Wakefield came from a long line of screamers.

Her Grandpops had screamed in the trenches during World War 1
while her dear Dad had screamed at Iwo Jima
and afterward in Korea.

As a young teen Jane first screamed at Elvis:
the 1960's saw her scream at The Beatles and The Stones.
In July 1971 the screaming stopped when Jim Morrison died.
In time Jane learned to scream again, firstly at Zeppelin
and when Bowie arrived on stage
she screamed so loud she nearly lost her voice!

In the 1980's Jane screamed at what society deemed
"more important things."
She screamed at politicians, bankers, devaluation, oil shortages,
nuclear threat, poverty and growing intensity and insanity of unjust wars.

Jane also birthed a fourth generation of screamers
and the family tradition and expectation continued into a new generation.

As the Millennium approached she reflected upon her screaming.
She thought perhaps that those who scream
ought to be the ones in government!

Find something to scream about.........

Part 4

2000 - Tomorrow

Tell Someone Today

BALTIMORE, MARYLAND - 2000

Love is a word easily used but its fruit is seldom worked on.

The tall spire and cold grey slate reflected the sheen from the overnight rain. Inside, the remains of Maryland resident, septuagenarian Edward Scole, had rested overnight in the reposing chapel of Baltimore's cathedral; his casket sitting under the watchful eye of stained glass and wood and stone statue. Nearer eleven the crowds converged to attend the funeral ceremony. The widows clasped beads and like at the dance hall the men, Ed's golfing buddies, stood on the opposite side to cast furtive glances at the prey. Winking and fidgeting, both sides shared memories of lighter moments.

The priest was an old friend. Father O'Malley, known as Popeye for his penchant for spinach and other assorted greens including the libations of the golf club's 19th, commenced the hour long formalities. Popeye filled the cavernous Nave with his incantations and platitudes while a retired colleague and friend eulogised. Popeye beckoned Edward's son Martin to share a memory but he, accompanied by his wife and teenage sons, declined; his only remark that he and his father had said everything to each other before his "old man" passed. Popeye directed the cortege toward the graveyard for burial; a quick service as the celebrant had a two o' clock tee time.

Like most funerals the solemnity was lost with the warming help of alcohol; the deceased forgotten by the second drink. Its the way Ed would have wanted it the attendees convinced themselves as the cat and mouse parry between widow and golfer commenced: it is a bad funeral that doesn't result in at least one marriage! Popeye left for golf and Martin and family left too. Nobody noticed.

On the way home Martin and family stopped by the graveyard and stood with reverence beside the new plot. A silent tear fell to rest upon the freshly turned and packed soil; Maureen clutched her husband's hand. She knew his pain.

"At the hospital Dad told me what his father told him on his deathbed," Martin said as he turned to his wife, "and as I've reflected, its something he said to me every day. He told me to tell those closest to me that I love them every day. He said that to Ma and me all the time; got a bit annoying but I get it now. Last thing he said to me you know. Wish I could hear him just once more."

Martin leaned over and kissed his wife as they walked toward the car for home.

Straight and Narrow

BOSTON, MASSACHUSETTS – 2003

Many don't make it to the other side of addiction.

She sat alone......waiting. It seemed to her that she had been alone all her life; even in company. She had been orphaned at a young age then abandoned by unloving relatives. A series of foster homes had followed; each change left an indelible damaging mark.

This, her third time in rehab, had come to an end and as she waited for release the chaos of the last decade made an attempt to assault her now calmed mind.

The first onslaught aims to panic and disorientate; a two pronged attack to disarm confidence and instil fear. Her mind filled with images and sensations of the past. First the physical nature of her ordeal screamed through her veins. The abuse, the first hazed escape to oblivion, the stealing, the arrests, the selling of her body and later her soul. This physical attack encroached further: the downward spiral to harder drugs, the seriousness of growing involvement in heinous crime, the overdose, the faint pulse and the first two failed attempts at rehab. The physical attack was difficult. From experience she knew that the emotional bombardment would soon follow and follow it did: the stress of her early loss, the abandonment and her gnawing anxiety, the denial, the utter shame and constant self-loathing. The barrier she erected to numb her feelings together with the concurrent desire to be a part of a loving and healthy family. The overwhelming need for safe friendship, acceptance and ultimately love; unconditional love with no expectation or need to payback heart given favour.

The last three months had given her the skill-set to identify all these triggers. This time she felt she could overcome and conquer these attacks driven by stealth and horror. This time she had hope.

She had been given different names all her life and sometimes she had been identified solely as a number. This time she had decided upon her own name. She wouldn't immediately accept the kind offer of a fresh start from a distant cousin. Instead from today she would work and save her own money in this her fresh start. Perhaps later she would avail of the offer but Boston was home.

She sat patiently, comfortable in her own company. When the buzzer rang the door automatically opened and Jennifer took her first tentative step outside.

Snoqualmie

WASHINGTON STATE 2008

Like nature, character is forged through adversity.

Wrapped in fierce rugged beauty,
formed in the caverns of the deep.
Earth's first scarring when
fervent heat, dirt and boiling water
exploded to majestic peak.
Now snow capped,
transcending field and cloud.
Glacial waters warming first to slow meander
then descending to white water rage,
plunging to booming fall.

Megan Cassidy had left the city;
its maddening pace and ego
long since consigned to the caverns of her mind.

Megan's hand painted red hulled kayak
made a gentle, comfortable pace.
Its bright colour stood in stark contrast to
the surrounding greens and blues of nature.
This hunting ground of the wild
announced its own early morning commerce.
Sounds of clamour,
bellow and winged hum,
rustle and insect bite.

Megan no longer cared for the activities of industry
her conscience telling her of a liberty
now desired by those highway commuters passing by;
those fixated by politic and restless gain.

Untamed Snoqualmie, birthed in chaos yet distilled to peace:
a shared history with Megan Cassidy.

$18,000,000 over Thirty Years

WILMINGTON, DELAWARE – 2014

No matter what you do somebody somewhere will make money out of you.

The last second of life is the longest of times but mostly the worst of times: a lifetime of memory and thought often cascade into consciousness. Some memories can be good, even funny and some are not; things that were said, secrets that should have remained unspoken.

The same occurred for Ron Stevens, an army veteran and seventeen year traffic cop with the Wilmington Police force. So used to pulling over speeding and other infraction offenders, Ron didn't fully see the gun that ended his life. The random thoughts came quick, too quick for his brain to process. Unfortunately Ron's reactions were also too slow.

"Man, I was going to have steak for dinner."
"I shouldn't have said that to Kyle this morning." Kyle was his twelve year old.
"Least Amy will have my pension and she was going to leave me anyway."
"Listen. I can hear the birds sing. What a beautiful sound."
"Wonder will they ever catch this son of a .....?"
"All the money I've generated for this State; $300 an hour, everyday." Work the math like Ron did each night: over a thirty year stint its $18 million.
"Two lousy weeks holiday a year. Bloodsuckers!"
"When I was 17 I really loved Michelle."
"I liked the army, though the war was tough. Didn't like the killing but the friends were good. I should have kept in touch.....least with some of them."
"Man I hated living here and I loved living here. It is close enough to the big cities for a day out and yet far enough away to keep safe."
"Go Jets.....Go!!"
"I should have married Michelle. Why didn't I chase her down?"

"Just three years to my pension and golf every day."
"Joe owes me $5........man he never pays up!!"
"Glad I repented."
"This second seems like its lasting forev..............

Ron was buried with full police honours. The following Monday morning Jayne Weathers took Ron's job.

"$300 an hour; $18,000,000 over 30 years....." the new recruit was a bright lady; she worked it out on her first night.

Utopian Wrestling of Smith's Mind

CONNECTICUT – 2015

**My great friend Fhesty is going through this.
He is stronger than their nonsense.**

Smith felt like he had worked for dead men for almost 30 years; dead pillars of salt, moving breathing automatons working to expected patterns of behaviour. Men and Women with no emotion, people who had lost their souls: individuals in collective groups that had tried, with varying degrees of success, to rob Smith of his humanity. Most of these "colleagues" had sacrificed family for career.

Attracted to the world of academia at a young age, Smith spent years at study before landing a teaching assistant's job in one of America's Ivy Leagues. The years passed and tenure was eventually awarded: the result of hard work, ceaseless publishing and politicking.

Smith discovered that his world was not the world captured in glossy brochures, rather it was a world of subterfuge, intrigue, blinding ambition, rank, intellectual superiority, political alliance, collusion with fraternal society and relationship with the banking elite; legacy guaranteed for a dollar amount.

Smith looked from his window onto manicured lawns, fond memories of his mentor flooding his mind. His mentor had walked the hallowed halls for four decades always pointing Smith toward his vocational responsibility. Now in his mid-fifties and divorced Smith once again pondered important questions. Is it an educator's responsibility to harness and develop critical thinking or to socially engineer young minds? Is it right to financially entice and ensnare the next generation and then graduate them as indentured slaves into a corrupt banking system? How do you best promote a national working ethos delivered by character, integrity and service to others like Smith thought the founding fathers had done? How do you balance a budget without attaching a monetary value to a human being? How do I answer these fundamentally critical questions while holding venomous thoughts about those I work with? Smith had internalised so many questions but had thus far manifested so few answers.

Smith's mother had warned him about his probing mind; "seems like she was right," he chuckled. He yearned for a 1962 Steinbeck adventure in his own "Rocinante", instead he reached for a Whiskey; a small luxury before delivering his well researched debate provoking afternoon tutorial.

Resignation Letter

ARLINGTON, VIRGINIA – NOVEMBER 2016

Procrastination has ruined the integrity of many.

For three days the carefully crafted handwritten but unmailed letter had stared back blankly from his mahogany polished desk. Theodore S. Prentice thoughtfully nudged the sealed envelope with his right hand; the fingers of his left tapping nervously on his knee. If mailed it would change the course of an illustrious family history. He recalled the content, word for word.

Dear Mr. President,

It has been my privilege to serve as Chief Executive of Polaris Security Incorporated for the last twenty five years. As you know I am the tenth generation heir of a company founded by my late ancestor Mr. Walter Prentice during the Presidency of Thomas Jefferson in 1801. Together The White House and Polaris celebrated our bicentenary and commenced the third century of our prosperous union.

Our shared relationship charts the history of our noble and esteemed nation. The initial wooden fence of 1801 was, seven years later, replaced by stone. An iron fence and stone piering was constructed a decade later. Post civil war improvements were again commissioned and in 1873 President Grant expanded southward with enclosed iron. Post World War One our honorable President Coolidge continued to permanently close off our Nation's Residence with further work. After Pearl Harbor, Polaris improved defences prior to our entry into the globe's second war. Stone re-inforcements were constructed in the 1970's; similar barricades erected in the 1980's. This current century saw further enhancement post September 2001 and yet again last year.

As I survey the passage of time I acknowledge that Polaris has flourished, but at what cost to our citizens; to those who have toiled relentlessly to build these United States. Our Forefathers committed the self-evident truth that all men are created equal to our Declaration of Independence. As I observe I recoil that "We the People," has been replaced by "We the Corporation." With each lost life and outpouring of blood the body politic has become further removed and distant to those who vote for the incumbent of America's highest office. Each step further away from those we serve another brick and iron bar was added to the ground.

It is with a heavy heart that I sit here. From my desk I can see Arlington Cemetery and stare across the great Potomac toward our Nation's Capital and it is from the writing place of my ancestors that I commit pen to paper. In full acknowledgement of the countless Presidents we have served I now, in my own hand, confirm the resignation of Polaris forthwith.

Yours Faithfully.

Theodore S. Prentice.

The perplexed Theodore sighed. His conscience affirmed his wrestled thoughts: but what about the family pocket? What about the future; his own legacy?

He slowly removed the letter from his desk and locked it in his drawer.

"Perhaps I will send it tomorrow," he assured himself. "Yes, tomorrow."

Just a $10 Buck Joad

NEW JERSEY – MARCH 2020

Covid 19 – To the soon forgotten frontline workers who mostly earn minimum wage.

She left her meth-head cheater and her only kid,
trailer park tincan down a dead end street,
a walk to the bus stop else hitch a ride,
other side of tracks to her working life.

Hungry, broke, skin-pinched, forlorn,
job as a cleaner, rich frightened at home,
she mopped and she polished floor tile and chrome,
$10Bucks for her efforts she worked to the bone.

The virus came fast they said it wouldn't last,
it was the $10Buck heroes kept the country going,
the unnamed, unloved modern day slave,
making their dollar, paying their way.

2020 should be two good eyes,
need a government with vision not one to despise,
they took our taxes built their trophies and smiled,
workers weary beaten, tired red eyes.

It's a difficult season things sure have changed,
make a few calls, share some grace,
chat to your neighbour, carry their load
pray to The Lord this time end soon.

She left the hospital at the end of her hours,
worried bout germs lest she bring them home,
song on the radio, bus driving its load
she soon figured out she just a $10Buck Joad.

No Rules to this Dance

MANHATTAN, NEW YORK - TOMORROW

For many it all becomes about mammon.

The yellow pulled curb side.
$45 he growled nastily.
I dropped a Fifty; he barked.
I flipped a middle finger and exited.
My feet hit East 58th Street and Madison.
This is my domain.

An immediate atomic assault.
Waves of steel and grind;
tumultuous, frenetic.
Suits emerging from subway steam,
street hawkers, screamers, dealers,
ranters on corners pushing their wares.
Egos demanding their rite of passage,
a regular Darwinian stampede.
Trucks n cars,
horn like symphonies.
Blue Cop whistles,
each note llooonngg n slow
adding to the chaotic confusion.

Glass n girders punching the sky.
I entered a gleaming tower of Babel,
pushed the button to 75.
Overlooking a small patch of central green
like who gives a ....whatever!

Meeting table,
shouting and roaring,
pens in the place of hammer cocked Colts,
heavyweight blows; left n right.
Revenge extracted,
handshake........no feeling.
I departed quickly,
cheque in pocket, five zeroes in tow.
Bruised not beaten.
Brain reeling.

Confident on the out,
turn them to my back
consigning them to the past.
Another rain spotted yellow to quayside.
Ferry, only half hour to home.
Mind racing.
Mental note: must practice my aggression to blunt out the soft!
More tomorrow..........I'll get it too!
Manhattan........ love it, hate it..... it's still Manhattan.
Gotta love it!

Other books by Redmond Holt

Testimony: Onward toward salvation.

Mammon

Eulogy: Jerusalem 70AD.

dystHOPEia.

Are you inspired to write a book?

Contact

Maurice Wylie Media
Your Inspirational & Christian Book Publisher
Based in Northern Ireland, serving readers worldwide

www.MauriceWylieMedia.com

www.ingramcontent.com/pod-product-compliance
Lightning Source LLC
Chambersburg PA
CBHW040540170726
48295CB00012B/534